The Bravest Babysitter

The Bravest Babysitter

by Barbara Greenberg
pictures by Diane Paterson

The Dial Press   New York

4692711

Text copyright © 1977 by Barbara Greenberg
Pictures copyright © 1977 by Diane Paterson
All rights reserved / First Printing
Printed in the United States of America
Typography by Suzanne Haldane
Production by Ann Wallerstein
Printed by A. Hoen & Co. Inc.
Bound by Economy Bookbinding Corp.

Library of Congress Cataloging in Publication Data

Greenberg, Barbara, 1940-   The bravest babysitter.
Summary: Heather baby-sits for Lisa but they
switch roles when a thunderstorm frightens Heather.
[1. Baby sitters—Fiction. 2. Thunderstorms—Fiction]
I. Paterson, Diane. II. Title.
PZ7.G8272Br   [E]   77-71516
ISBN 0-8037-0363-5   ISBN 0-8037-0364-3 lib. bdg.

13·1·77 &LG 2·75

For my children, Lisa and Jeffrey
and my husband, Hank

The doorbell rang, and Lisa galloped over to help Mother open the door. Heather, Lisa's favorite babysitter, walked in. Heather bent down and said, "Hi, Lis. You got a haircut. Now I can tickle you right here on the back of your neck."

"What do you have on?" asked Lisa. She opened Heather's coat. Heather had come right from hockey practice. Under her long coat she wore short shorts. Purple and orange stripes chased each other around her knee socks.

Lisa always had a good time with Heather. Heather liked to read books aloud, and she laughed hard at the silly parts and made her voice spooky for the scary parts. She was good at drawing, and she called Lisa "Lis."

Mother left, and Lisa and Heather got to work on a collage. Lisa liked to paste bumpy and smooth and bright-colored things all together on paper to make a design. This time she got big macaroni and small macaroni and some white buttons and brown buttons and a big shiny gold one. Heather cut out pictures from a magazine.

It started raining while they were working on the collage. It was a rough windy rain. It beat against the house and rattled the windows.

Suddenly the darkness outside got white with light, and then thunder rumbled through the sky.

"Oh, no. Thunder!" said Heather. She dropped the scissors and held onto the arms of the chair. "Get ready. Here comes another one," she said after the next flash of lightning.

"What's the matter, Heather?" asked Lisa. "Are you scared?"

"Scared? Who's scared of a little thunder," said Heather when it was quiet again. "Now, listen, you thunder, you'll have to whisper please," yelled Heather.

Lisa laughed.

"Oh, no. Here comes more," said Heather. And she put her hands over her ears and squeezed her eyes shut.

"My mother always tells me to keep busy so I don't think so much about the thunder," Lisa said. "So let's paste."

Lisa pasted her big macaroni and small macaroni and her white buttons and brown buttons and her big shiny gold button on some paper. She loved sticking her fingers in the paste and making collages, and she didn't think about the thunder.

But Heather wasn't paying attention to what she was doing. She pasted a picture right onto the table instead of onto the paper.

"Oh, no," said Lisa. "Look what you did."

"Maybe we ought to eat supper now," said Heather.

"Okay," said Lisa. "And let's play restaurant."

They had hamburgers on buns and apple juice with straws—just like at Dan's Diner in town. While she was eating her hamburger, Lisa said, "Let's make believe I'm the waitress and you're the little girl."

She patted Heather on the head and said, "Now you eat up all of that good hamburger, honey. Don't spill the sugar on the floor, we'll get ants."

"What did you say?" asked Heather.

Heather hadn't heard a word, and she hadn't eaten a bite.

"Let's think of something else to do," said Lisa. "Do you want to read me a story?"

Lisa and Heather snuggled together in the soft armchair in the living room. Heather read a story.

There was a blaze of lightning and a bang of thunder. Heather sank lower into the chair and pulled Lisa down with her. Heather went on reading, but she didn't laugh now at the silly parts or make her voice spooky for the scary parts. She read and then looked out of the window and then read again and looked out of the window again. She kept losing her place.

"Let's play dress-up instead," said Lisa at last, and she dragged out her box full of old clothes. She draped a shawl around her shoulders, and she put a floppy hat, piled high with cherries and feathers, on her head. She pulled out a long dress and gave it to Heather.

But Heather got all tangled up in the dress. First she put one arm where the head should go. Then she put her head where the arm should go. Finally she put it on right.

Then Lisa pulled out a pair of shoes and gave them to Heather. But Heather put the shoes on the wrong feet.

There was another flash of light. Then *rumble, roar, crash,* went the thunder.

"That was a loud one," said Heather.

"It will stop soon," said Lisa.

"You're brave, Lis," said Heather.

"Let's draw with crayons," said Lisa.

Lisa drew a picture of a sunny day with red and yellow flowers and green stems and a big, round, orange sun. Heather drew a picture of a rainstorm with a streak of lightning across the sky.

"I like yours better," said Heather.

"Here. It's for you," said Lisa.

It was Lisa's bedtime. She put on her pajamas and got ready for bed. But Heather said, "You may stay up tonight until the rain stops. Let's keep each other company a little while longer."

"Sometimes when there's thunder outside, my mother puts on a record and we dance," Lisa said.

Lisa and Heather chose a record and played it loud. Heather loved to dance. When she danced, her long hair flapped against her back. Lisa hopped and jumped and tumbled on the floor, but she couldn't get her short hair to flap like Heather's.

When the record was over, Heather said, "Look, it's stopped raining. There's no more thunder. You'd better go to sleep now. Would you like me to tuck you in?"

"No," said Lisa. "I'll tuck myself in tonight."

"You're a very good babysitter, Lis," said Heather.

"I know," said Lisa. "I hope there's thunder the next time you come so I can take care of you again. I like being a babysitter."

BARBARA GREENBERG, a former elementary school-teacher, was born in the Bronx. For two years she lived in Cameroon, Africa, where she taught at the international school. She has worked with modern dance groups in Boston and New York. Ms. Greenberg now lives outside New York City with her husband, a cardiologist, and their two children. She teaches creative dance to four- and five-year-olds and writes for the County Symphony of Westchester Lollipop Concert Series. This is her first book.

DIANE PATERSON is the author/illustrator of several books including *Eat!*, *Smile for Auntie*, and *If I Were a Toad*, the latter two Junior Literary Guild Selections, and the illustrator of *Monnie Hates Lydia* (all Dial). Ms. Paterson lives in Ridgefield, Connecticut, with her husband and two children.

576 1 05